SPORTS ON THE EDGE!

EXTREME SNOWBOARDING

Daniel Benjamin

Marshall Cavendish Benchmark
New York

Copyright (C) 2012 Marshall Cavendish Corporation
PUBLISHED BY MARSHALL CAVENDISH BENCHMARK
AN IMPRINT OF MARSHALL CAVENDISH CORPORATION
ALL RIGHTS RESERVED.

NOTE FROM THE PUBLISHER:
Do not attempt this sport without wearing proper safety gear and taking safety precautions.

No part of this publication may be reproduced, stored in a retrieval system or transmitted, in any form or by any means, electronic, mechanical, photocopying, recording, or otherwise, without the prior permission of the copyright owner. Request for permission should be addressed to the Publisher, Marshall Cavendish Corporation, 99 White Plains Road, Tarrytown, NY 10591. Tel: (914) 332-8888, fax: (914) 332-1888.

Website: www.marshallcavendish.us

This publication represents the opinions and views of the author based on Daniel Benjamin's personal experience, knowledge, and research. The information in this book serves as a general guide only. The author and publisher have used their best efforts in preparing this book and disclaim liability rising directly and indirectly from the use and application of this book.

Other Marshall Cavendish Offices:
Marshall Cavendish International (Asia) Private Limited, 1 New Industrial Road, Singapore 536196 • Marshall Cavendish International (Thailand) Co Ltd. 253 Asoke, 12th Flr, Sukhumvit 21 Road, Klongtoey Nua, Wattana, Bangkok 10110, Thailand • Marshall Cavendish (Malaysia) Sdn Bhd, Times Subang, Lot 46, Subang Hi-Tech Industrial Park, Batu Tiga, 40000 Shah Alam, Selangor Darul Ehsan, Malaysia

Marshall Cavendish is a trademark of Times Publishing Limited

All websites were available and accurate when this book was sent to press.

LIBRARY OF CONGRESS CATALOGING-IN-PUBLICATION DATA
Benjamin, Daniel, 1960–
Extreme snowboarding / Daniel Benjamin.
p. cm. — (Sports on the edge!)
Includes bibliographical references and index.
Summary: "Explores the sport of extreme snowboarding"—Provided by publisher.
ISBN 978-1-60870-229-9 (print) ISBN 978-1-60870-749-2 (ebook)
1. Snowboarding—Juvenile literature. I. Title.
GV857.S57B455 2012
796.939—dc22
2010039534

EDITOR: Christine Florie   PUBLISHER: Michelle Bisson
ART DIRECTOR: Anahid Hamparian   SERIES DESIGNER: Kristen Branch

EXPERT READER: Paul Krahulec, USASA regional series director,
U.S. Snowboard Sports Committee

Photo research by Marybeth Kavanagh

Cover photo by *Flirt/SuperStock*
The photographs in this book are used by permission and through the courtesy of: *SuperStock:* Flirt, 1, 3; All Canada Photos, 4, 18; IndexStock, 11; The Copyright Group, 28; Aurora Open, 40; *Newscom:* Andrew Malana/Icon SMI 767, 9; *PhotoEdit Inc.:* Jonathan Nourok, 15, 29; *Getty Images:* Greg Ceo, 19; Doug Pensinger, 23; Photo and Co, 26; Joe Kohen/WireImage, 32; Cameron Spencer, 36, 42; *Photolibrary:* Adrian Myers/Cultura RM, 17; *Alamy:* Peter Llewellyn, 30; StockShot, 38; *Landov:* Roger L. Wollenberg/UPI, 34

Printed in Malaysia (T)
1 3 5 6 4 2

Contents

ONE
SURFING ON SNOW — 5

TWO
GETTING READY — 12

THREE
GETTING ON YOUR BOARD — 22

FOUR
THE GREATS — 31

FIVE
WHERE SNOWBOARDING GETS EXTREME — 37

GLOSSARY — 43
FIND OUT MORE — 44
INDEX — 46

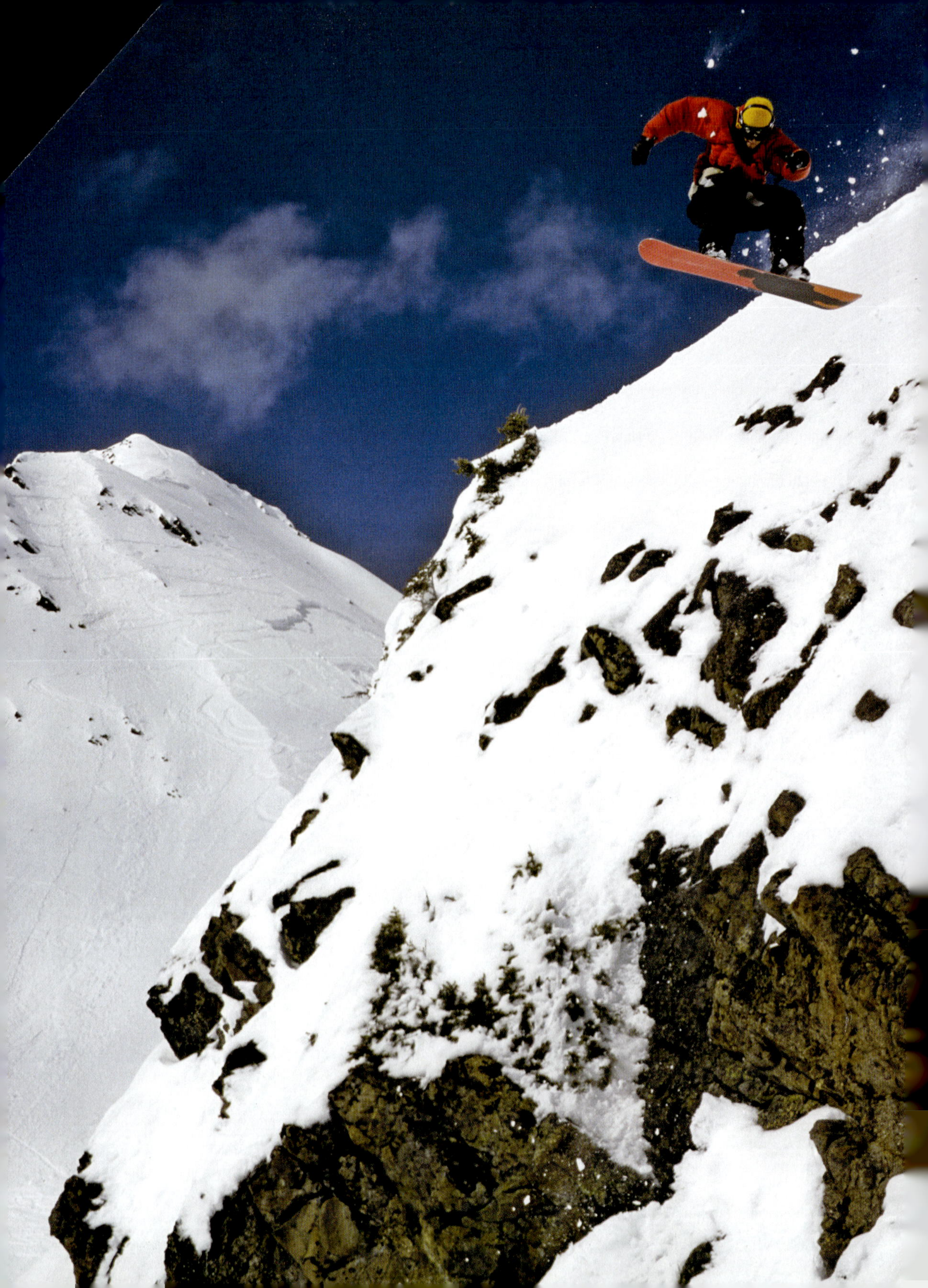

ONE
SURFING ON SNOW

MOST CURRENTLY POPULAR winter sports have been around for centuries. Pictures of the first skiers appear on rock drawings made in Norway five thousand years ago. People from that time also used ice skates made from animal bones to travel across frozen water in the winter. But you won't find any rock art of athletes whooshing down snowy hills like surfers on **fiberglass** boards. This sport, born in the modern age, is called snowboarding.

⟵ THIS SNOWBOARDER "GOES EXTREME" OFF A CLIFF AT BANFF NATIONAL PARK IN ALBERTA, CANADA.

Forty years ago snowboarders didn't exist, except for a few early pioneers. Thirty years ago many U.S. ski areas didn't allow snowboards on their slopes. Today, most mountains attract more snowboarders than skiers. While most riders stick to marked trails, others "go extreme," taking their boards up the sides of unmarked mountains (sometimes getting there by helicopter), then whooshing down steep inclines, in and around trees, and through fresh powder. These extreme snowboarders share a special thrill: they are often the first to board down sections of the world's most difficult terrain. But extreme snowboarding is a risky sport. Even the most experienced snowboarder can accidentally trigger an avalanche. As one rider puts it, "If you want to go extreme on a board, you've got to be experienced and very careful. But strap in, 'cause it's a wild ride!"

The First Snowboarders

Who was the first person to strap a board to his or her feet and rocket down a snowy hill? Records from the 1920s show that some adventurers raced down mountains with their feet tied to pieces of plywood. Needless to say, "plywood-boarding" didn't catch on.

Today, most experts credit Sherman Poppen, a chemical engineer from Muskegon, Michigan, with creating the first snowboard. On a winter day in 1965, Poppen tied together two skis and then tied a rope to their tips for the rider to hold for steering as he or she went down a hill. As his daughter, Wendy, glided down a hill in their backyard, his wife dubbed the new contraption a Snurfer. Soon, all of Wendy's friends wanted one, and Poppen got busy manufacturing more of them. Poppen sold more than half a million Snurfers in the United States in a single year for $15 each. Poppen even took to organizing small Snurfing competitions.

Despite the Snurfer's popularity, future snowboarders were still searching for a better board. In 1969 an East Coast surfer named Dimitrije Milovich discovered the joys of sliding down icy hills while standing on a school cafeteria tray.

Soon, Milovich hooked up with a surfboard maker named Wayne Stovekin. In 1971 they started to manufacture snowboards roughly based on surfboards, but with metal edges. In the course of the next decade, other enthusiastic inventors such as Mike Olson, Tom Sims, Chuck Barfoot, and Jake Burton Carpenter experimented with their own boards. But outside of a small group of snowboarding enthusiasts, the sport was still waiting to become popular with the wider public.

Snowboarding Comes on Strong

In 1979 a snowboarder named Paul Graves alerted sports enthusiasts around the world to the potential of these new boards. Appearing in the last Snurfer contest, held in Michigan, Graves made every second count, pulling off a dazzling array of flips, as well as four sliding 360-degree turns.

In 1982 Graves organized the first national snowboarding championships. Held at Suicide Six Ski Area in Woodstock, Vermont, the event was

The First Great Snowboarder

EVERY SPORT HAS its legends. Born in Norway in 1974, Terje Haakonsen has been called "the Michael Jordan of snowboarding," dominating the sport by winning (among other contests) the International Snowboard Federation (ISF) World Championships in the half-pipe three times in a row, in 1993, 1995, and 1997.

Haakonsen also made a name for himself by refusing to compete in the 1998 Winter Olympics in Nagano, Japan, which was the first Olympic Games to include snowboarding. Haakonsen's complaint was that the International Olympic Committee had given authority over snowboarding events to the Fédération Internationale de Ski (FIS) instead of to the snowboarders' own organization, the ISF. Haakonsen and other snowboarders maintained that the FIS had little understanding of snowboarding culture, which favors the individual joy of popping a great new trick over winning trophies. Despite missing out on an almost certain Olympic medal, Haakonsen is still considered the greatest early snowboarder in the sport's history.

covered by *Good Morning America* and the *Today Show*, which filmed contestants tearing down the mountain on early snowboards and Snurfers. Soon, the sport was attracting hordes of teenagers who hit the slopes in baggy skateboard clothing. But as the sport caught on, some skiers objected to the more free-spirited snowboarders, who often left ruts in the trails. Many ski resorts hung up NO SNOWBOARDING signs. It wasn't until 1986—when the World Snowboarding Championships, held in Breckenridge, Colorado, brought press and money to the city—that ski resorts finally began to share their trails.

Snowboarding Today

Today, snowboarding is one of the fastest-growing sports in the world. Not only is it the most popular winter sport among teens, it is also popular with some older enthusiasts who have switched from skis to snowboards. At the same time, new stars are grabbing headlines. In the days leading up to the 2010 Winter Olympics in Vancouver, Canada, U.S. snowboarder

SNOWBOARDERS CATCH AIR AS THEY JUMP OFF AN OVERHANG IN COLORADO.

Shaun White appeared on the cover of the popular magazine *Rolling Stone*. His defense of his gold medal in the half-pipe competition was one of the most watched events of the games.

As snowboarding has become more mainstream, more riders have pushed the limits of the sport. The best extreme snowboarders are so skilled that they can ride down an almost vertical mountain and catch air off small cliffs. The sport can also be extremely dangerous—great snowboarders often compare injuries—but the rewards are great. This book can get you started on your way down the hill.

TWO
GETTING READY

PERHAPS IT'S OBVIOUS, but snowboarding isn't something you can do in your driveway. Of course, if you have a backyard with a good hill, you can try out your new snowboard at home. But if you want to get into more serious riding, you're going to have to find a board and boots, get yourself to a ski slope, purchase a lift ticket, and maybe even pay for a lesson. All this can make snowboarding an expensive sport to start. The good news is that if you have the funds to invest in the right equipment and a season lift ticket, the rest of your expenses will be pretty manageable. And as snowboarders around the globe will tell you, it will be money well spent.

Your First Time on a Board

Ready to whoosh down a mountain? Actually, there are some important decisions to make before you get to the slopes at all. These have to do with your equipment, specifically the snowboard, boots, and **bindings**. Perhaps the most important decision of all sounds the strangest: are you regular or goofy?

No, this does not refer to whether you like to board while pretending to be a cartoon dog. Rather, it refers to the foot you will place in the forward position on your board. The best way to choose is to take off your shoes and slide across an uncarpeted floor in your socks. Whatever foot naturally goes forward is the one to put up front on your snowboard. If it's your left foot, you are a "regular" rider. Those snowboarders who place their right foot forward are called "goofy" riders. Another way to figure out your natural board position is to stand still and have a friend give you a light shove from behind. Whatever foot goes forward to break your fall is the foot you should put forward on your board.

What to Wear

SNOWBOARDING CAN BE a cold pastime. Here is a quick guide on how to stay warm on the slopes.

WEAR LONG UNDERWEAR made from a polyester blend.
BUY A GOOD PAIR OF SKI SOCKS.
IN WARMER WEATHER many snowboarders like to wear hooded sweatshirts. But be warned: on cold days, the hood will freeze solid—not a cool look.
WEAR A LIGHTWEIGHT FLEECE JACKET in warmer weather.
WEAR A DOWN JACKET when it's very cold.
BUY A GOOD HELMET.
USE SUNSCREEN.
WEAR GOGGLES.

THIS SNOWBOARDER IS A "REGULAR" RIDER. HER LEFT FOOT IS IN THE FORWARD POSITION.

Snowboards come in three basic heights: short, medium, and long. In general, short boards, which measure from the floor to around the rider's collarbone, are easiest to ride. Medium boards, used by intermediate riders, come between a rider's chin and nose. Long boards come up to the rider's eyes and are used by serious snowboarders who want to pick up major speed in deep powder.

The width of your snowboard relates directly to your foot size. If you have a big foot, you'll need a wider board. If your feet are small, you'll need a narrower board. If your foot is too small for your board, you won't have much control over it. If your feet are too big for your board, your boots will catch on the snow and cause epic wipeouts.

Snowboards today can be divided into three major categories, based on three different kinds of riding. The most common type of snowboarder rides a freeride board. **Freeriders** are boarders who make use of the whole mountain and enjoy every aspect of the sport, from whooshing down the hills to catching air. A **freestyler** spends most of his or her time working on tricks, jumps, spins, and rail sliding at a snowboard park. Freestyle boards are generally shorter and are made for use with softer boots that are specially designed for doing tricks. Finally, there are **carvers** who like to board like they ski—they make hard turns at high speeds down a mountain. Carve/alpine boards are longer, harder, and use a stiffer boot to give riders greater control in powder. Most beginner snowboarders use a freeride or freestyle board to start.

Snowboard boots are a lot like ski boots—they are large and heavy and are designed to hold your foot firmly in a binding so you can cruise downhill without twisting your ankles. The fact that snowboard boots are heavy doesn't mean they have to be uncomfortable. Though most boots break in over time, it's a good rule of thumb to make sure your boots feel pretty good the very first time you put them on. Make sure each boot fits snugly but comfortably around your

A FREESTYLER'S BOARD IS SHORTER THAN OTHER BOARDS AND DESIGNED FOR TRICKS SUCH AS RAIL SLIDING.

heel and ankle, with your toes just touching the inside tip of the boot. The correct fit will prevent your heel from sliding up off the sole of the boot and your foot

17

SNOWBOARD BOOTS ARE SIMILAR TO SKI BOOTS. THEY'RE BIG, HEAVY, AND MADE TO SUPPORT YOUR ANKLES.

from sliding forward. On the other hand, if there's too much pressure on your toes, ankles, or tops of your feet, you should move on to a different pair. In the end, color, style, model, and what your best friend likes don't matter. Try on different brands and different sizes, lace them up completely, and then buy the boots that fit your feet best. Comfortable boots can mean the difference between a great day in the snow and a painful one.

Once you've got your boots, you're ready to look for bindings, which will attach your boots to your board. Look for bindings with padded straps, as they are usually the most comfortable. Bindings with metal ratchets (on the part that tightens onto your boot) usually last longer than plastic ones and won't break in cold weather as easily.

To find the right bindings, you'll need to figure out your stance, or your position on the board. First, you need to decide how far apart you want to keep your feet. One easy rule of thumb is to stand with your feet at shoulders' width apart. Then you'll have to choose where to put your feet on the board. If you're going to be doing **park riding** and tricks,

BEFORE YOU ATTACH BINDINGS TO YOUR BOARD YOU MUST KNOW YOUR STANCE— THAT IS, THE PLACEMENT OF YOUR FEET ON THE BOARD.

Learning the Lingo

MORE THAN MANY SPORTS, snowboarding has its own lingo. Here's a brief guide to some commonly used terms.

MCTWIST a 180-degree turn with a front flip
INDY GRAB a trick in which a snowboarder bends down and grabs the part of the snowboard that is between the feet after hitting a jump
JIBBING sliding on a rail, box, tree stump, or any other feature lying on the snow
MISTY FLIP a 360-degree front flip
NOSE GRAB a trick in which a snowboarder brings the feet up to the right side and grabs the front tip of the snowboard
TAIL GRAB a trick in which a snowboarder brings the feet up to the right side and grabs the back tip of the snowboard
CATCHING AN EDGE digging an edge of the board into the snow (when this happens, it usually causes a fall)
SHREDDING riding a snowboard

you'll want a center stance—feet in the middle of the board—so you have maximum control over the board at all times. Riders who want to bomb down slopes covered in deep powder often prefer their stance to be further back on the board so their front end doesn't get buried in snow. Finally, make sure your feet are centered on the board. If your heel or toe juts out too far over the side, your foot might catch snow and flip you off the board.

Choosing equipment might seem confusing. Don't forget that salespeople are trained to help you. Go to a snowboard shop, and tell an expert how experienced you are and what kind of riding you want to do. He or she will outfit you properly. Then you'll be ready to hit the hills.

THREE
GETTING ON YOUR BOARD

On my first day snowboarding... I was like most people, on my hands and knees crawling around a bunch. But the main thing that I remember is that I could go and have fun and do whatever I wanted.

—Snowboarder Jeff Anderson

SO YOU HAVE a new snowboard. You've figured out whether you'll ride regular or goofy and have bought or rented a pair of snug, comfortable boots. Now you're ready to pull off some spectacular leaps on the local half-pipe.

BEFORE HITTING THE SLOPES, TAKE A FEW SNOWBOARD LESSONS.

Maybe not quite yet. While you don't have to be a super jock to learn how to snowboard, it'll probably take a little practice before you're able to bomb down a hill. Expert rider Joe Curtis says it best: "If there's one thing I'd say to a first timer, it's to go out and get a lesson." Nothing beats one-on-one instruction from a pro. Getting the right advice up front can save you wipeouts later. (But don't forget rule number one of snowboarding: everyone wipes out sometimes.) If you can't afford a lesson, ask an experienced friend or grab someone who looks like he or she knows what to do and ask for help. In the meantime, here are some basics.

Snowboard Etiquette

HERE ARE SOME rules of the trail.

Ride within your abilities. Stay in control.
Always give people ahead of you on the trail the right of way.
Don't stop where you might block the trail.
After stopping, look uphill to avoid a collision before you start riding again.
Use a security leash (a rope that attaches your binding to your boot) to prevent your board from flying down the mountain if you fall.
Follow all warnings and signs.
Never duck under a rope.

Before you strap in with both feet, get comfortable with having a single foot in the binding. First, find a flat area with packed snow. With your front foot buckled in and your back foot to the side of the board, practice lifting the board up and down. Easy? It may not be at first, but once you feel balanced moving your board with a single foot, you're ready to skate. To do that, push off with your back foot, and let the board slide forward. Take small steps at first. As you get more comfortable, push harder, place your free foot on the back of your board, bend your knees, and glide.

After you've learned how to skate and glide, bind your free foot to the board. Find a small hill, and stand carefully with the side of your board facing down the mountain. Hold yourself in place by digging your heel edges into the snow. Then, when you're ready, gradually release some of the pressure on your heels. You should start to slip down the mountain sideways. When you feel comfortable sideslipping forward, turn around so your back is facing downhill. Gradually release the pressure on your toes and slide again. Yes, you'll be moving backward, but don't panic. If you get going too fast, just dig in with your toes. And be sure to look over your shoulder so you can see where you're going.

Once you're ready for real hills, you'll need to learn how to turn. Experts are able to whoosh straight down the **fall line**. But traversing, or going back and forth across, a mountain allows you to control your speed as you become more comfortable on your board. To begin, stand at the top of a hill as though you were going to sideslip down on your heels (or forward side). Then jump a bit so your board points down the hill at an angle. As you start to slide, keep your weight on your back edge. Once you've reached the opposite side of the hill, stop by digging in with your heels. Then turn around and try to traverse the slope from the left to the right, stopping yourself by digging in with your toes.

When snowboarding, there are two basic turns to master. Heelside is a turn to the right. Toeside is a turn to the left. As in skiing, making a turn

THIS SNOWBOARDER MAKES HEELSIDE AND TOESIDE TURNS ON HIS WAY DOWN A MOUNTAIN SLOPE.

comes down to bending your knees and shifting your weight in the direction you want to go as you glide down a hill. If you want to turn to your right on a snowboard, dig your heels slightly into the snow, and you will begin to turn right. To stop, dig your heels in deeper. Likewise, if you want to turn left, push down with your toes and look left.

Some Basic Tricks

More than most sports, snowboarding is an activity that celebrates an individual's creativity. The best boarders like to make up tricks as they go. Even so, there are some basic tricks that most snowboarders learn after they've found their legs.

Riding **switch** is snowboard lingo for riding backward. It's actually easier than you may think. The trick is to keep spinning around as you go into a turn until your front foot is now your back foot. It'll feel weird the first few times, but you'll get used to it sooner than you think. All good snowboarders ride switch every now and then.

Then there's a 360 ground spin. That's when you turn yourself around in a full circle and keep on going down the hill. To try it, push hard into a turn, and keep on pushing. About halfway around, you may start to slow down. Dig in with your heels, and push yourself all the way around.

Ever done a wheelie on a bicycle? Popping one on a snowboard is similar. After you've picked up some speed, place your weight on your rear foot. Then pull up your board's front tip as hard as you can.

Finally, all serious snowboarders can do an **ollie**, a leap into the air used either to have fun or to jump over obstacles. To do it, perform these next steps in one smooth and quick sequence.

THIS SNOWBOARDER POPS A WHEELIE, A BASIC SNOWBOARDING TRICK.

1. Pull your front foot up hard, and load your weight onto your board's tail to use it as a spring.
2. Pop off your back foot while lifting your back leg and drawing your knees up as high to your chest as you can, so you level off the board.
3. Straighten your legs as you come back down, but bend your knees slighly to absorb the impact of the landing.

MANY SNOWBOARDERS LEARN HOW TO DO OLLIES, WHICH ARE BASIC JUMPS.

A SNOWBOARDER CATCHES AIR AS SHE COMES UP THE SIDE OF A HALF-PIPE.

THE HALF-PIPE

So what is a half-pipe, anyway? Basically, it's a great place to have fun and to try out serious tricks. Most half-pipes are ramps that are about 330 feet long. The walls are about 18 feet high, with a distance of 59 feet between them.

Before you try to turn yourself into the next Shaun White, start slowly. Traverse carefully up the sides of the half-pipe, and then turn and board back down. Once you gain some confidence, do a little hop at the top of the pipe as you turn. The next time, push off harder. As you're airborne, turn your body to face back down into the half-pipe.

The good news is that the better you are at doing basic tricks on the slopes and in the pipe, the better you'll be out on the extreme hills. Practice hard, and you'll be ready for pretty much anything the most difficult mountain will throw at you.

FOUR
THE GREATS

NOW THAT WE'VE GONE over the basics, let's take a look at some of the best extreme riders on the slopes today.

Travis Rice

Born in 1982 in Jackson Hole, Wyoming, Travis Rice has been called the Paul Revere of the big mountain freestyle revolution. As fellow rider Victoria Jealouse puts it, "Travis is an all-around rider of the sickest" stuff.

A skier and hockey player as a boy, Rice switched to snowboarding as a teen. In 2001 Rice came out of nowhere to wow the snowboarding world when

TRAVIS RICE MADE A NAME FOR HIMSELF IN THE SNOWBOARDING WORLD IN HIS EARLY TEENS.

he landed what is known as a back-side rodeo off a 110-foot gap jump at Mammoth Mountain, California. After that, Rice appeared in a series of snowboard videos in which he proved he was one of the best. He famously jumped 120 feet over Chad's Gap, in Utah, while doing a 540 (a rotation and a half in midair).

In 2008 Rice coproduced and starred in *That's It, That's All*, a film that features some of the sport's biggest names. For the film Rice nailed a double cork 1280—three complete spins in midair—while keeping his head tucked below his waist on each rotation. It was a trick that helped get Rice named rider of the year. As fellow rider Eddie Wall puts it, Rice is the "gnarliest guy ever."

A Sport on Video

MORE THAN ANY other athletes, the great extreme riders of today spend a chunk of their time shooting movies of their sickest tricks. One of the best-known is *First Descent*, produced in 2005, in which Terje Haakonsen, Travis Rice, Shaun White, and Hannah Teter ride across some of Alaska's most difficult terrain.

Today, *Snowboard Magazine* comes out with an annual list of the best videos. And snowboarding has inspired an array of video games that simulate boarding down a steep hill. The first, released in 1990, was *Heavy Shreddin'*. More recently, a game called *Shaun White Snowboarding: World Stage* celebrates the famous Olympian.

Hannah Teter

The best-known American woman snowboarder of the past ten years, Hannah Teter has done it all. She has won Olympic medals in the half-pipe as well as at the Winter X Games, where athletes show off their more extreme skills. Hailing from Belmont, Vermont, Teter was born into a family of snowboarders. Two of

HANNAH TETER EARNED A SILVER MEDAL FOR SNOWBOARD LADIES' HALF-PIPE AT THE 2010 WINTER OLYMPICS IN VANCOUVER, CANADA.

her older brothers, Abe and Elijah, have ridden for the U.S. Olympic team, and her oldest brother, Amen, is her agent. Still, it didn't take long for Hannah Teter, who started riding at age eight, to prove she was the best in the family. At age fifteen she was the world junior half-pipe champion. In 2006, while recovering from a knee injury, she won the Olympic gold medal in half-pipe. In 2010 she won the silver medal. In 2005 Teter costarred with snowboarding legends Shaun White and Terje Haakonsen in *First Descent*, one of the best-known extreme snowboarding films ever shot.

As impressive as what Teter has done on the snow is what she has done off it. Wanting to use her celebrity for social good, in 2008 she founded Hannah's Gold, an organization that raises money for clean-water projects and schools in Kirindon, Kenya, through the sale of Vermont maple syrup. In 2009 Teter donated all of her prize winnings to the foundation.

Shaun White

The best snowboarder of his generation, Shaun White is also one of the world's best skateboarders. Over the past decade White has chalked up an awesome record. He became the first person in history to win medals in the Winter X Games (in snowboarding) and Summer X Games (skateboarding) in the same year. He won gold medals in half-pipe in the 2006 and 2010 Winter Olympics. White has won a medal in the Winter X Games every year since 2002.

Nicknamed the flying tomato because of his long red hair, White remains at the top of his sport. In 2009 Red Bull, his chief sponsor, built him his own private half-pipe on Silverton Mountain in Colorado. It is reachable only by helicopter, so he can work on his new tricks in private. And what tricks they are! White has been the first to land many of the sport's most extreme maneuvers. Perhaps his most famous is the

SHAUN WHITE STOPS FOR A PHOTO AFTER WINNING THE MEN'S SNOWBOARD HALF-PIPE IN 2009 IN NEW ZEALAND.

Double McTwist 1260, which he nailed to win the gold medal in the 2010 Olympic Games. A mind-boggling combination of three twists and two flips, it left NBC commentator Todd Richards sputtering for a way to describe it: "[It's] the Double McTwist," he shouted. "The Big Mac. Whatever you want to call it. The Whitesnake. The Double Double Extra Tomato. I don't care what you're going to call it, that was unbelievable."

Nailing new tricks and riding down new, treacherous paths is part of what makes snowboarding so much fun. Shaun White is still in his mid–twenties, so anyone interested in the sport should see a lot of him for years to come. Next time you're at a half-pipe, look up in the air. He might be the blur with long red hair that's flipping over your head.

FIVE
WHERE SNOWBOARDING GETS EXTREME

SO WHERE DO the most extreme riders of all go to strut their stuff? The answer is anywhere there's a steep mountain that no one has ridden before. While snowboarding remains a sport in which the individual rider's goal is to stretch his or her own limits, there are times when the world's best riders throw down to see who is the sickest of them all.

The Avalanche

THERE'S NO DOUBT that extreme snowboarding can be a dangerous sport. Riders can fall and break bones. But the biggest danger by far is accidentally triggering an avalanche. If a rider travels across an area with unstable snow, he or she can trigger an avalanche. Avalanches occur when the buried layers of snow can no longer support the snow on top of them. A shredding snowboarder can be the trigger that sets the layers of snow in motion down a slope. Avalanche survivor John Verity describes how quickly it can happen: "I thought a lot of snow kicked up, then I looked around and saw that the whole [mountain] face was going and I was in the middle of this slide. It really started building up speed quickly and I tried to stand and ride out, but it was too fast and the snow hit me from behind. I flipped over onto my front, and it just got darker and heavier."

Luckily, Verity's partner was able to find him and dig him out before he suffocated. Today, all extreme snowboarders ride with a shovel, a probe for finding the exact location of buried people, a first-aid kit, and an avalanche beacon that transmits a signal to rescuers from under the snow.

King of the Mountain: Valdez, Alaska

The best extreme snowboarders have shredded slopes all over the world. But most riders would say that the best of all is in Valdez, Alaska. The city is best known for lending its name to the supertanker that caused a disastrous oil spill in 1989. But snowboarders know Valdez for something else: its incredible mountains. In fact, snowboarders view the Valdez slopes with a respect that borders on awe. "There's nothing better than taking a helicopter to the top of these mountains, then going down as fast as your body and gravity will take you," one rider says. "This is the best in the world." Another describes mountains "just lined up to the horizon." Valdez is the place where the best riders go to test themselves.

It's also the site of King of the Hill, the best-known extreme boarding competition. And how tough are the mountains? The first competition, held in 1992, only lasted one run. As the King of the Hill website puts it, the rest of the three days were "about

THE BEST AND MOST EXTREME SNOWBOARDERS RIDE THE MOUNTAINS OF VALDEZ, ALASKA.

respecting these mountains with your friends." It goes on to add, "Nobody died."

Even so, riders have come back to test their skills at King of the Hill year after year. Competitors participate in two events. The downhill is a timed 4,000-foot vertical run. The freestyle is a 3,000-foot run that includes small cliffs and natural half-pipes, and it is picked by a panel of judges. Just what are those judges looking for? A number of factors go into choosing the winner:

⇨ the rider who takes the most difficult path down the mountain
⇨ the rider who exhibits the most control
⇨ the rider with the best style and tricks
⇨ the rider who is the most aggressive going down the hill

Winners in 2010 included superstar Travis Rice and one of the best upcoming extreme riders, German boarder Vera Janssen. The mountains are frightening, to be sure, but for the best in the world, Valdez is the ultimate test. As one rider put it, "It's a do-or-die situation for some, a party for others, and the chance of a lifetime for most."

The World Heli Challenge Ski and Snowboard Festival

Probably the second most important event on the extreme snowboarder's calendar is in faraway New Zealand. At the World Heli Challenge ski and snowboard festival, the best riders in the world compete over a two-week period for prizes in extreme and freestyle boarding. The goal is to determine the athlete with the skills to traverse very steep terrain and to perform the coolest jumps and tricks. To make sure the competitors have the best chance to truly strut their stuff, the competition is held over a nine-day period, but snowboarders only ride on the

SHIN BIYAJIMA OF JAPAN COMPETES AT THE 2010 WORLD HELI CHALLENGE IN WANAKA, NEW ZEALAND.

three days when the snow conditions are deemed to be the best. In 2010 many of the world's best snowboarders competed, including Travis Rice.

The Future of Snowboarding

Looking back, it's stunning to see just how fast snowboarding has swept the world. Forty years ago, Dimitrije Milovich was snowboarding down hills on a cafeteria tray. Today, most ski areas have a half-pipe or a terrain park for snowboarding. At the same time, extreme riders keep finding newer and higher mountains to conquer. What other sport combines speed, tricks, cool lingo, and a never-ending string of eye-popping videos? Whether extreme or on a marked trail, snowboarding is here to stay.

What are you waiting for?

GLOSSARY

bindings the metal or plastic latch that holds the boarder's foot in place on the snowboard

carver someone who likes to snowboard like a skier, taking deep turns down the mountain

fall line the fastest way down a slope

fiberglass a material made from extremely fine fibers of glass that is used to make snowboards

freerider a snowboarder who enjoys all aspects of the sport, from whooshing down mountains to popping tricks

freestyler a snowboarder who focuses on executing tricks and jumps

half-pipe a 330-foot-long, U-shaped ramp with 18-foot sides in which a snowboarder performs tricks

ollie a front leap in the air while riding down a mountain on a snowboard

park riding a course set with obstacles where a snowboarder can work on trick maneuvers

switch riding a snowboard backward

FIND OUT MORE

BOOKS
Gitlin, Marty. *Shaun White: Snow and Skateboard Champion*. Berkeley Heights, NJ: Enslow, 2009.

Jacobellis, Lindsey. *Extreme Snowboarding with Lindsey Jacobellis*. Hockessin, DE: Mitchell Lane Publishers, 2008.

Schwartz, Heather. *Snowboarding* (Science Behind Sports). San Diego, CA: Lucent Books, 2011.

DVDs
1st Step: The Ultimate Snowboard Trick Tip Series. 2003.

Burton Snowboards: For Right or Wrong. VAS, 2007.

WEBSITES
Snowboarding.com
www.snowboarding.com
    This site includes links to equipment, clothes, snowboarding news, and thrilling videos.

United States Ski and Snowboard Association

www.ussa.org

    This site includes information on the USSA's sports, events, and news.

U.S. Snowboarding

www.ussnowboarding.com

    The website of the U.S. Olympic snowboarding team includes information about the sport.

INDEX

Page numbers in **boldface** are illustrations.

avalanches, 38, **38**

Banff National Park, **4**
basic tips, 24–27
basic tricks, 27–29, **28, 29**
bindings, 19, 43
board position, 13, **15**
boots, 17–18, **18**

carvers, 16, 43
clothing, 14
culture of snowboarding, 9

equipment, 12–13, 14, 15–19, 21
etiquette, 24

fall line, 43
Fédération Internationale de Ski (FIS), 9
fiberglass, 43
films, 32

First Decent, 33
foot position, 13, **15**
freeriders, 16, 43
freestyler, 16, **17,** 43

Graves, Paul, 8

Haakonsen, Terje, 9, **9**
half-pipe, 30, **30,** 43
Hannah's Gold, 34–35

International Snowboard Federation (ISF), 9

King of the Hill, 39–41

lessons, 23
lingo, 20

Milovich, Dimitrije, 7–8

ollie, 28–29, **29,** 43

Olympic Games, 9, 10–11, 34, 35, 36

park riding, 43
Poppen, Sherman, 7

Rice, Travis, 31–32, **32**

snowboard inventors, 7–8
snowboard styles, 15–16
Snurfer, 7, 8
stance, 19, **19,** 21
Stovekin, Wayne, 8
Suicide Six Ski Area, 8, 10
Summer X Games, 35
switch, 27, 43

Teter, Hannah, 33–35, **34**
That's It, That's All, 32
360 ground spin, 28
turns, toeside & heelside, **26,** 26–27

Valdez, Alaska, 39–41, **40**

Verity, John, 38
videos, 33

wheelie, 28, **28**
White, Shaun, 10–11, 35–36, **36**
Winter X Games, 33, 35
Woodstock, Vermont, 8, 10
World Heli Challenge, 41–42, **42**
World Snowboarding Championships, 10

47

ABOUT THE AUTHOR

DANIEL BENJAMIN is the author of many nonfiction books for children. His other title in Marshall Cavendish's Sports on the Edge! series is *Extreme Mountain Biking*. He lives in New York City with his wife and two children.